Anna, Banana,

and the
Monkey
in the
Middle

Anna, Banana,

and the
Monkey
in the
Middle

Anica Mrose Rissi

ILLUSTRATED BY Meg Park

SIMON & SCHUSTER
BOOKS FOR YOUNG READERS
New York   London   Toronto   Sydney   New Delhi

SIMON & SCHUSTER BOOKS FOR YOUNG READERS
An imprint of Simon & Schuster Children's Publishing Division
1230 Avenue of the Americas, New York, New York 10020
This book is a work of fiction. Any references to historical events,
real people, or real places are used fictitiously. Other names, characters, places,
and events are products of the author's imagination, and any resemblance to actual
events or places or persons, living or dead, is entirely coincidental.
Text copyright © 2015 by Anica Mrose Rissi
Illustrations copyright © 2015 by Meg Park
All rights reserved, including the right of reproduction in whole or in part in any form.
SIMON & SCHUSTER BOOKS FOR YOUNG READERS
is a trademark of Simon & Schuster, Inc.
Also available in a Simon & Schuster Books for Young Readers hardcover edition
Book design by Laurent Linn
The text for this book was set in Minister Std.
The illustrations for this book were rendered in digitally.
Manufactured in the United States of America
0517 0FF
First Simon & Schuster Books for Young Readers paperback edition July 2016
2 4 6 8 10 9 7 5 3
The Library of Congress has cataloged the hardcover edition as follows:
Rissi, Anica Mrose.
Anna, Banana, and the monkey in the middle / Anica Mrose Rissi ;
illustrated by Meg Park.
pages cm
Summary: Anna has looked forward to her class field trip to the zoo, but from the
time they board the bus she is pulled between her long-time best friend, Sadie, and
new best friend, Isabel, who argue about everything and want Anna to take sides.
ISBN 978-1-4814-1608-5 (hc)
[1. Best friends—Fiction. 2. Friendship—Fiction. 3. Behavior—Fiction. 4. Zoos—
Fiction. 5. School field trips—Fiction. 6. Family life—Fiction. 7. Dogs—Fiction.]
I. Park, Meg, illustrator. II. Title.
PZ7.R5265Ans 2015
[Fic]—dc23
2014017618
ISBN 978-1-4814-1609-2 (pbk)
ISBN 978-1-4814-1610-8 (eBook)

For Sophia Jane
(and Tessie, too)
—A. M. R.

For Donna and Maggie, my Sadie and Isabel
—M. P.

Anna, Banana,

and the
Monkey
in the
Middle

Chapter One
Rise and Shine

I popped up like a jackrabbit-in-the-box, feeling wide-awake and eager as a beaver. I had animals on the brain.

"Banana!" I said, leaning over the side of my bed. "We're going to the zoo!"

Banana looked up at me with her big doggy eyes and thumped her tail against the pillow in her basket where she sleeps. I reached down to tug her soft ears. She understood, of course, that by "we" I didn't mean her and me—dogs aren't allowed on school field trips. I meant me and my best friends, Sadie and Isabel, plus the rest of our class and the other two third-grade classes. It was going to be a super fun day.

"I wish I could sneak you there in my backpack," I said. "Then you could meet the prairie dogs!"

My teacher, Ms. Burland, had shown us pictures of prairie dogs and some of the other animals we'd be seeing at the zoo. We'd learned what the animals eat and how they play and other cool things about them. I liked hearing about the animals' habitats, like where they sleep and what parts of the world they're from. Ms. Burland says the animals that live in a place are part of what makes that region unique. ("Unique" had been our word of the day. It means special and different and one of a kind.) That made a lot of sense to me. Banana definitely makes my house unique, and my room is extra special because she sleeps there.

"But actually," I told her as I slid out of bed, "prairie dogs are in the squirrel family, not the dog family. So if I took you to the zoo, you'd probably want to chase them."

Banana wiggled in agreement. She loves chasing squirrels.

"They're called prairie dogs because they bark like dogs," I said. "And because they live in the prairie. Except for the ones that live at the zoo."

Banana yawned and stretched her front legs. I guess she'd heard enough facts about prairie dogs.

I made my bed and pulled on my outfit of black leggings, a pink-and-white striped shirt, pink sneakers, and black-and-white polka-dot socks. While I got dressed, I sang a silly song that Isabel had made up. "We're going to the zoo! A-doob-a-doob-a-doo! We're going to the zoo! You and me and you!" Yesterday at recess, Isabel and I had linked arms and skipped around the playground, belting out the song at the top of our lungs. We'd stopped short when I'd noticed Sadie watching us with her arms crossed and her eyebrows worried. We hadn't meant to leave Sadie out. It had just happened. Luckily, Isabel had grabbed on to Sadie and soon we were all three skipping and singing, and Sadie looked happy again. But it had been a close call.

Sadie and I have been friends forever, but we only just met Isabel this year. It's twice as much fun having two best friends, and mostly, we all get along great. But in some ways Sadie and Isabel are still getting used to each other, I think. I was glad we would have the whole day at the zoo to have fun as a threesome. Banana and I were certain that by the end of the field trip, Sadie and Isabel would be calling each other "best friend" too.

I grabbed my backpack off the floor and a note fell out of the side pocket. I unfolded the paper and saw it was a drawing Isabel had made of two cute pandas chewing on bamboo. She'd written *Anna* under one of the pandas and *Isabel* under the other. The pandas even kind of looked like us. Isabel is an amazing artist.

I smiled at the drawing and taped it up on my mirror, under a photo strip of Sadie and me goofing around in a photo booth. "There," I said to Banana. "How does that look?"

Instead of answering, Banana pounced on her favorite plastic bunny toy and shook it back and forth, growling as it squeaked. I laughed. Banana is just a little wiener dog but I think in her head she's as huge and ferocious as a tiger. A tiger that likes to cuddle in my lap, and sometimes spins in circles, chasing her own tail.

"Come on, crazy beast," I said. "Time for breakfast."

I put on a headband and my gold pony necklace with the sparkly blue eye, and galloped out the door.

Chapter Two
Monkeying Around

When we got to the kitchen, Dad was already there, sipping coffee from his TOP DOG mug and making a cheese-and-pickle sandwich for my lunch. "Hey, kiddo," he said. "And hey, Banana."

I gave Dad a good-morning hug, scooped some kibble into Banana's food dish, and poured myself a big bowl of Gorilla Grams. "I'm going to see a real gorilla at the zoo today!" I told Dad.

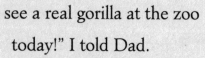

My brother, Chuck, poked me in the ribs. "Kind of like how you see a real monkey every time you look in the mirror?" he said.

"Better than when you look and see a giant slug," I shot back. Chuck snorted into his orange juice.

Dad looked like he might start a lecture on teasing, so I quickly distracted him with cool animal facts. "Did you know that gorillas can weigh over four hundred pounds?" I asked. "They're huge!"

"Wow," Dad said. "I did not. Must be all those Gorilla Grams they eat for breakfast."

"Nope," I said, even though he was kidding. "They eat roots and leaves and tree bark and fruit. And also *slugs*." I stuck out my tongue at my brother.

"Mmmmm, slugs," Chuck said.

Banana licked the kibble crumbs from her snout and trotted over to her usual spot at my feet. She sat and looked up at me with perked ears and hopeful eyes, wondering if I might drop my food. Sadie calls that Banana's "Please?" position. Isabel hasn't gotten to see how Banana acts at breakfast yet, but maybe we'd all have a sleepover soon. Then Banana could beg at Isabel's feet too.

Mom came into the kitchen wearing her Important Meeting Suit. Her shoes clicked on the tile floor as she walked over to kiss Dad on the cheek and take the mug of coffee he held out to her. She even *sounded* important.

Mom works in a big office where she's the boss. Everyone there has to do what she says, except for the clients, who get to tell Mom what they want, and she and her team try to make them happy. That's what Mom calls the people who work for her, her "team." It sounds like they should be wearing matching uniforms with numbers on the back and doing stretches together and stuff, but they wear regular office clothes like Mom's and mostly just sit at their desks.

Sometimes I go to the office with Mom, and everyone who works there is super nice to me. Mom's assistant, Mr. Max, lets me use his fancy pens and highlighters. I draw pictures to put up in people's cubicles, and string paper clips into crowns and necklaces for Mr. Max and me to wear.

The necklace Mom had on with her suit this morning wasn't made of paper clips, but it was still pretty. "You look powerful," I said.

She laughed, even though I was serious. "Thanks, Annabear. I have a big day today. And so do you! Are you ready for all those hippos and zebras?"

I danced in my seat. "Yes!"

Banana wagged her tail but Chuck made a grumpy face. "It's no fair that Anna gets to go play with monkeys all day and I have to take a stupid math test."

"Sure it's fair!" I said. "You got to go when you were in third grade. And I've never been to the zoo yet."

"Yes you have." He pointed at me with his spoon. "Where do you think we got you from? Dad and Mom found you in the Monkey House."

I knew that couldn't be true, but I looked at Dad to make sure. He shook his head. "He's teasing, Anna," Dad said. "Chuck, we're going to send *you* to the Monkey House if you don't stop torturing your sister."

"Yeah, send me to the Monkey House!" Chuck said. He jumped around, scratching his armpits and going, "Oooh-oooh-oooh-oooh!"

"Maybe *after* your math test," Dad said. Chuck fell back into his chair.

Dad opened the cupboard and took out a box of fruit strips. He dropped a cherry one into my lunch bag.

"May I have three?" I asked. "*Pleeeeeeeease?* To share with Isabel and Sadie?" I made wide, pleading eyes like Banana's when she begs. I tried to lift my ears like she does too.

It worked! Dad dropped two more fruit strips into the lunch bag. "Sharing is good," he said. "Just don't share your fingers or toes with the lions, okay?"

I drew an X across my heart to make it a promise. "I won't," I said. But I couldn't wait to share the lunchtime surprise with my friends.

Chapter Three

Faster Than a Speeding Turtle

I finished my breakfast and glanced at the clock. It was time to go!

I jumped up, quick like a bunny, and raced to the sink with my dishes. I dashed up the stairs, fast as a cheetah, and brushed my teeth with hummingbird speed. Banana's ears flew behind her as we zoomed back downstairs. I kissed her on the nose and went out the front door.

Chuck and I started down the sidewalk, but he was in no hurry to get to school. If he walked any slower, he'd practically be moving backwards. He really didn't want to take that math test.

"Come on, come on!" I said, pulling his arm. It was like trying to drag an elephant. "Hurry up, slowpoke!"

"Chill, Annabean," he said, sounding all grumbly. But he moved a little faster.

I *had* to be on time. Ms. Burland had said that

if anyone was late, the buses would leave without them, because it wasn't fair for one person to hold up the whole group. There was no way I was going to get left behind and have to spend the day alone in the school library instead of at the zoo with my friends. It would be horrible to miss out on seeing the animals, and even worse knowing that Sadie and Isabel were having all that fun without me. What if it was so fun that they didn't even miss me?

I sped up.

Finally, we got to school and I saw the two yellow field-trip buses parked near the edge of the playground, just like Ms. Burland had said they would be. Ms. Burland and the other teachers were there too, lining up the kids who had already arrived. I spotted Sadie's bouncy curls and Isabel's cute braids. My friends were waiting!

I held on to my backpack straps and broke into a run. "Good luck with your test!" I called back over my shoulder to Chuck. He gave a funny salute.

"Hi!" I said as I reached my friends. I was panting a little from running. "I thought I might be late!"

Sadie and Isabel made room for me in the line. "We wouldn't have let them leave without you," Sadie said.

Isabel looked just as excited as I felt. "We're going to the zoo! To meet a kangaroo! And know what else we'll do? We'll see a panda, too!" she sang. Isabel loves making up silly songs.

"Thanks for the panda drawing!" I said. "It's super cute. Banana likes it too."

Isabel gave a shy smile. Sadie scrunched up her face. "What panda drawing?" Sadie asked.

Before I could answer, someone behind me said, "Hey, Anna."

I turned around. *Uh-oh*. It was annoying Justin.

"What's gray and has four legs and a trunk?" he said.

Sadie put her hands on her hips. She's always up for a challenge. "That's easy," she said. "An elephant."

Justin smirked. "Nope! A mouse on vacation!"

I rolled my eyes, but Sadie giggled. She thinks Justin's cute.

"Well, what's gray and has three trunks, four tails, and six legs?" Sadie said.

Justin's eyes narrowed. "What?" he asked.

"An elephant with spare parts!" Sadie said.

"Nice," Justin said. Sadie glowed.

I thought of one. "What do you call an elephant that needs a bath?"

"Trouble?" Isabel guessed.

"Nope," I said. "A smellyphant!" I'd have to remember to tell Banana that joke. Dogs like anything smelly.

Sadie nudged me. "How about this: What's black and white and pink all over?"

I smiled. I knew the answer she was thinking of.

"I've heard that one," Justin said. "A blushing penguin."

Sadie put her arm around me. "Nope!" she said. "*We* are."

Sadie was wearing pink, black, and white today too. We hadn't planned it that way, but Sadie and I have been friends for so long that sometimes things like that happen. We wear the same colors on the same day, or have the same idea at the same time, or know what the other one is thinking before she even says it.

"We're twins!" Sadie said. "Can you tell us apart?"

As I slid my arm around Sadie's waist, I noticed Isabel standing off to the side, staring at the ground. She looked sad and left out. But I knew how to fix it.

I took the pink headband off of my head and placed it on Isabel's. "There!" I said. "Now we're triplets." It wasn't quite true, but Isabel still looked pleased.

Justin shook his head. "Girls are so weird," he said.

But we didn't care. Now everyone could see that we belonged together.

Chapter Four

Hop to It

The bus doors squeaked open and everyone lunged forward, eager to board first.

"C'mon!" Sadie took charge, pushing into the herd of kids. "Let's get a good seat!" she said. I followed her closely, with Isabel right behind me.

Ms. Burland stood next to the bus door, towering over everyone like a giraffe. "Nicely, nicely! No need to shove," she called out. "I don't want to see any animal behavior until we get to the zoo. And then I only want to see it happening *inside* the cages."

There were some groans, but people stopped pushing and got back in line. Ms. Burland can be strict, but she's still the best teacher in the whole Lower School. Even Justin listens to her and does what she says. Usually.

Isabel tugged on my sleeve. "We're sitting together, right?" she asked.

"Of course!" I said, just like I'd said yesterday when Sadie had asked the same thing.

We reached the front of the line and Ms. Burland checked off our names on her clipboard. I looked down at her feet. "Wow! Nice shoes," I said. She wore glittery purple high-tops with white toes and white laces. Banana would love them. She always likes hearing about Ms. Burland's cool shoes.

"Thanks!" Ms. Burland said. She did a little dance and the sneakers sparkled in the sun.

I climbed up the stairs onto the bus and followed Sadie down the aisle. She grabbed a seat as far back as we could go, and scootched over toward the window to make room. I slid in after her and squeezed over too, so Isabel could sit on the end. There was just enough space for all three of us.

But the second Isabel's butt hit the seat, we heard the bus driver shout, "Two to a seat!"

"Oh no!" I said, looking at Isabel, then at Sadie, then at Isabel again.

"But we fit!" Sadie protested.

"I don't care if twenty of you fit," the bus driver grumbled. "Two to a seat. Those are the rules."

Sadie fell back into the corner. "That's not fair," she said. "Grown-ups shouldn't get to just make up the rules. We should all get to vote on it." But I could see she knew there was no use in fighting it. And I supposed the rule *was* fair if it was the same rule for everybody.

"What are we going to do?" I said. I didn't want one of us to have to sit alone or with some other kid. I wanted us to stick together, like we'd planned.

I wished that I could have brought Banana. At least then we could have divided up into two and two.

Sadie grabbed my arm. "You said yesterday

you'd sit with me," she said. "You promised."

Isabel's eyebrows shot up. "You said you'd sit with me, too!"

Oh no. "I want to sit with both of you!" I said. "I wasn't lying. I just didn't know."

"Well, you have to decide," Sadie said, still clutching my arm. "You can't sit with us both."

Isabel nodded grimly. We all knew it was the truth.

They waited to hear my choice. But I couldn't decide anything. My brain was frozen, like a deer in headlights.

What was I supposed to do?

Chapter Five

Split Decision

The bus was filling up fast. I needed to decide quickly, before there were no good seats left for whoever had to move. But I didn't want either of my friends to go. And I definitely didn't want to have to choose who would.

If I chose Isabel, I knew Sadie would be upset. But if I chose Sadie, then Isabel would be upset. No matter what I did, someone was going to feel left out.

This was terrible.

Maybe I should be the one to go sit by myself. But that wouldn't make anyone happy either.

Then I'd be breaking my promise to *both* of my friends.

I wished I could shove my head in the sand like an ostrich, or hide under a blanket like Banana, and wait for the problem to go away. But I was going to have to decide.

I felt Sadie's grip on my arm get tighter. Her message was clear: *Choose me*. It's hard to say no to Sadie. And she was right that I'd promised her first.

I turned to Isabel. "I'm sorry, but Sadie asked yesterday."

Isabel blinked. "Okay," she said. I was worried she'd be angry, but she just looked sad, which was even worse. It felt awful to disappoint her.

"I'll sit with you on the way home, okay?" I said as Isabel stood up. She nodded.

Sadie opened her mouth to object to that, but then she shut it and nodded too. "That's fair," she said. But she didn't look happy about it.

Isabel smiled at us both, a real smile. "Hey! It's all right," she said. "We still get to spend all day together at the zoo."

"True," I said, grateful she wasn't making a big deal about it. If Sadie were in her position, she'd probably be pouting. If it were me, I'd probably be pouting too. But Isabel is easygoing like that. It makes being a trio way less tricky.

Isabel headed up the aisle. "Monica!" she called to a kid in Mr. Garrison's class. "Can I sit with you?" Monica hitched over and Isabel slid into her new seat.

Sadie pulled a loop of yellow string out of her

backpack and wove her fingers through it. "Let's play cat's cradle," she said.

"Meow!" I answered, and reached for the string.

Chapter Six
Bear-y Funny

The bus ride passed quickly. At first I was worried that Isabel might be feeling abandoned. I leaned into the aisle to check on her and saw she had her nose in a book. But when she heard me say her name, she turned around and crossed her eyes to make a silly face at me, and I knew that it was okay.

"We're getting close!" Sadie said, pointing out the window. We whizzed past some giant banners with elephants, pandas, and tigers on them.

The bus came to a stop in front of a tall iron gate. Everyone jumped out of their seats like a pack of kangaroos. I bounced off the bus with Sadie right behind me. We ran over to Isabel.

"I thought of a riddle for you," Sadie said to her. "What do you call a panda bear with no ears?"

Isabel tipped her head to one side, like Banana does when she's thinking. "What?" she asked.

"A panda b!" Sadie said, sounding gleeful. She knows Isabel loves pandas.

"Ha!" Isabel said. "That's smart." She and Sadie beamed at each other. I felt as pleased as Banana when she's given a treat, seeing them getting along. If I had a tail, I'd have wagged it.

I stared up at the marble lion that stood guard at the entrance. I peeked around the statue and saw the words WELCOME TO THE ZOO spelled out across the top of the gates. I couldn't wait to meet the animals that lived behind them.

I wasn't the only one eager to get inside. There was excited chatter all around us as the last few kids spilled off the buses. I spotted a kid from Mr. Garrison's class playing keep-away with Timothy's hat and Timothy leaping for it like Banana does if you hold a toy out of her reach. One of the teachers, Ms. Chung, saw it too and gave the kid a stern look. He made a face like, *What?* and batted his eyelashes, pretending to be sweet and innocent. Ms. Chung crossed her arms. The kid handed back the hat.

"Hey," Isabel said in a hushed voice. "Have you ever seen Ms. Chung with her hair down?"

I shook my head. So did Sadie. I'd only ever seen Ms. Chung with her hair wound up in a bun like it was now.

Isabel leaned in closer. "Monica said she heard that someone saw it down in a braid once and it was *loooooong*. Like, all the way down her back. So long, she can probably sit on it!"

"Wow," Sadie said, staring at the teacher. "It's like she's secretly Rapunzel!"

Isabel giggled. "Yeah, and she climbs down out of her tower every morning to come teach third grade."

"That makes her smarter than Rapunzel," I said. "Climbing down yourself is way better than waiting for a prince." My friends agreed.

"I wonder how many hours it takes to wash it," Sadie whispered.

Isabel turned to me. "If you had a braid that long, you could use it as a leash to walk Banana," she said.

That was funny to picture. "And I wouldn't need a quilt on my bed," I said. "I could just sleep under my blanket of hair."

"You'd get a lot of tangles, though," Sadie pointed out, practical as always. "No wonder Ms. Chung wears it up. Also, this way she won't trip on it." I grinned. Sadie is practical, but she's also silly.

We heard a sharp tweet and turned to see Mr. Garrison with a whistle in his mouth. He blew it again and everyone quieted down.

Ms. Burland clapped twice. "Okay, my class, over here!" she called.

I linked one arm with Isabel and the other arm with Sadie. We skipped toward Ms. Burland and sang out together, "Lions and tigers and bears, oh my!"

Chapter Seven

Roaring to Go

"First things first," Ms. Burland said. "We're going to learn a lot and have fun today, but remember, we are guests here at the zoo—guests of the zoo-keepers and staff, and guests of the animals. I expect you all to be respectful of your hosts and show them your best behavior." Her voice stayed serious but she winked as she added, "So no monkeying around."

I looked over at Justin, but his eyes stayed on Ms. Burland. He shoved his hands into his pockets and stood up straight.

Ms. Burland kept talking. "If any of you get

lost or separated from the group, I want you to go to the information booth in the main building. Tell them you're in Ms. Burland's class, and wait for me there. I will come find you."

I shifted my weight from one foot to the other, like Banana does when she's impatient to go outside. I wanted us to get through the rules and instructions so the fun could begin!

"But you're not going to get lost, I'm sure, because you're each going to pair off with a buddy," Ms. Burland said.

I heard the word "pair" and my stomach sank to my toes. *Sets of two. Not again!*

"You are responsible for keeping track of your buddy throughout the day," Ms. Burland continued. "And together you will be doing a project on whatever animal interests you most."

Sadie's hand shot up in the air. "Ms. Burland," she called. "Ms. Burland!"

But Ms. Burland wasn't even looking in our direction. "Your projects will include a class presentation and a written report," she said. "Whatever animal you choose, I expect to see you working well together as a team."

Isabel looked worried, but Sadie looked determined. Sadie wiggled her fingers above her head and shouted Ms. Burland's name again. Ms. Burland ignored her.

"However," Ms. Burland said, "there's an odd number of you, so I need one group to be a set of three."

Yes! I put my hand up too. My heart pounded with hope. Beside me, Sadie waved her whole arm to get Ms. Burland's attention. "Ooh! Ooh!"

she said, sounding a lot like Chuck's monkey impression. "We will, Ms. Burland!"

Ms. Burland finally noticed us. "Okay, Sadie and Anna and Isabel, thanks for volunteering. You'll be our special threesome," she said.

My breath whooshed out in a sigh of relief. Thank goodness Sadie had reacted so quickly. It would have been terrible for us to be separated all day.

"Any questions while we wait for our guide?" Ms. Burland asked. I raised my hand again. "Yes, Anna?" she said.

"Do we still get a word of the day?" I asked. Every morning in our classroom, Ms. Burland writes a word of the day on the whiteboard. It's one of my favorite things about school. I love learning new words.

"Suck-up," our classmate Amanda muttered in front of me. Sadie glared at her and Amanda turned right back around.

"I'm glad you asked," Ms. Burland said. Her approval felt warm, like a sunbeam.

Ms. Burland leaned forward like she was about to share a secret with us. "The word of the day is 'scat'," she said. "S-C-A-T. One of its meanings is *go away*! If someone is bothering you, you might tell him or her to scat."

"Scat," I whispered toward the back of Amanda's head. It was a fun word to say. And useful.

"But scat has another meaning that we'll be seeing a lot of today," Ms. Burland said. "It's also a word for animal poop." She wiggled her eyebrows at us. "Sometimes when a tiger scats, he leaves his scat behind."

Even Amanda had to giggle at that. I bet now she thought the word of the day was cool.

"Let's all say it together," Ms. Burland said.

"SCAT!" we cheered. Some kids in the other classes looked over. I was proud that our class was the one having the most fun.

A lady dressed in khaki pants and a blue collared shirt walked over to our group. She was carrying a long pole with a bright green flag at the top, and her shirt had the zoo logo on it. She looked very official.

Ms. Burland introduced her to the class. "This is

Leticia. She's going to be our guide for the day."

Leticia gave us a wide smile. I liked her already.

"Hi, everyone," she said. "Welcome to the zoo. Come on and follow me inside!"

Chapter Eight

Drop with a Plop

We followed Leticia and her green flag in through the gates of the zoo and down a tree-lined path. She turned and said, "First stop: the Elephant House!"

We stepped inside. "It smells like horses!" Sadie said. I sniffed the air. She was right! The Elephant House smelled a lot like a stable—like sawdust and hay and manure. Isabel wrinkled her nose at the scent, but Sadie and I love horses, so for us it's a happy smell. If Banana were with us, she'd probably want to roll in it.

Even though I could smell the elephants, I couldn't see them yet. There were too many people in front of us. I stood on my tiptoes and stretched my neck, trying to peek over Amanda and her buddy, Keisha. All I could see was one elephant ear.

Isabel and Sadie slipped past Amanda and Keisha and Timothy and Justin. "Come on, Anna!" Isabel called.

I dodged around the other people and ran to join my friends at the fence. "I saved you a spot," Isabel said, motioning to a space next to her. But at the same time, Sadie said, "Anna, over here!" and pointed to a spot next to *her*, on the opposite side.

I froze for a second, not sure where to go. Then I realized what Banana would do if she were there. I nudged my way in between my friends, creating a new spot for myself in the middle.

I held on to the railing and looked into the pen. "Wow," I said. "Elephants are enormous!" I'd known that they would be, but it was still amazing to see it. Their toenails were the size of baseballs. Their butts were as wide as a car, with skin even more wrinkly than my Nana's. Only their eyes were small.

Three of them stood side by side, in front of a big door. They were swinging their tails back and forth like Banana does when she waits by her food dish, hinting that she'd like to be fed. "I bet they're hoping the zookeepers will come through that door with some food," I said.

I liked that there were three elephants, just like there were three of us. I wondered if the one in the middle had to worry about keeping both his friends happy, or if it was easier being an elephant threesome.

"That one looks like he's dancing!" Sadie said, pointing at the elephant closest to us. He shuffled his giant feet from side to side, swaying his whole body from the skinny tail to the long, low-hanging trunk. Even his ears were flapping along.

"My little cousin dances like that when she needs to pee," Isabel said.

"Maybe they're all waiting in line for the bathroom," I joked. Just as I said that, the middle elephant pooped! My friends and I burst into giggles.

"*That* one's not waiting," Sadie said. We laughed even harder.

I heard Justin shout, "Bombs away!" and Timothy yell back, "Scat attack!" as another elephant pooped too. Ms. Burland definitely had chosen the right word of the day.

"There's plenty more where that came from!" a loud voice behind us said. "Come see."

Chapter Nine

More Than Meets the Eye

We turned. Our guide, Leticia, was holding up a large ball of something suspiciously brown. I had a feeling it was not a mud cake.

Sadie let out a surprised yip. "Is that what I think it is?" she asked, stepping back to move away from it.

"If you think it's dried elephant dung, then yes!" Leticia said.

A couple of kids said, "Ew!" but Leticia didn't look at all embarrassed to be touching it. "'Dung' is one of the words that zookeepers use when we're talking about the animals' poop," she

explained. "And we talk about dung a lot around here, especially in the Elephant House."

Leticia had definitely caught everyone's attention. Keisha's mouth hung open in an O, and even Amanda looked impressed.

"Elephants are herbivores that love to eat,"

Leticia said. "An elephant in the wild eats between three hundred and five hundred pounds of food every single day. And what goes in must come out. So as you can imagine, each elephant produces a whole lot of dung—over a hundred pounds per day."

Wow. I was glad I had Banana instead of a pet elephant. A pet elephant would need a lot more walks.

"You can learn a lot about an elephant by studying its dung," Leticia said. "It tells you not only what he's been eating, but also how healthy he is. You can even look at his poop and figure out his age! The older the elephant, the larger his droppings. And scientists use the dung to study the elephants' hormones and DNA."

Isabel said, "Cool!" just as Sadie said, "Gross!"

They laughed and looked at me. I smiled but didn't say anything. I thought it was cool too, but I didn't want to agree with one of my friends over the other.

Leticia held out the dung ball. It was just a few inches away from us. "Take a closer look," she said to the class.

Sadie shrieked and ducked behind me. "Anna, protect me!" she said, like she was a princess and I was the dragon slayer.

Isabel stepped behind me too and said, "No, shield me!" just as dramatically, even though she's never squeamish. I guessed she was just playing along. They giggled together and peeked out at the monster poop. I liked being chosen as their hero, but I also felt almost left out of the game.

"I promise it won't hurt you," Leticia said.

I leaned in to look. Leticia explained that since elephants mostly eat plants, their dung is mostly made of plants too. That means it's not as stinky as a carnivore's poop.

Banana was not going to believe that this was what I was learning at the zoo.

"You have a few more minutes to look around here, and then we're off to the Ape House," Leticia told the class. "We've got lots of other animals to visit today!"

"Let's check out the displays," Sadie said, pulling me away from the elephants.

But at the same time, Isabel said, "Ooh, look!" and tugged me in the opposite direction.

"Ack!" I cried. "Wait!"

Isabel and Sadie froze, each holding one of my stretched-out arms. I felt ridiculous.

"You're going to rip me apart!" I said.

"Hey, good idea," Sadie joked. "Pull harder, Isabel. Then we each get half!"

Sadie and Isabel yanked on my limbs, pretending they wanted to split me in two. I knew they were just goofing around. It was funny.

But part of me worried it was also a little bit true.

Chapter Ten

Three's a Crowd

All morning, it kept happening. Sadie and Isabel kept choosing opposite sides on everything. And I kept getting caught in the middle of it.

In the Reptile Room, Isabel thought the snakes were beautiful, but Sadie shivered at the way they slithered and slid. In the amphibian area, Sadie said the yellow tree frog was cutest, but Isabel liked the tiny blue

one best. I pretended not to hear when Sadie asked what I thought.

In the Bird House, we made up a song about parrots. Isabel rhymed "birds of a feather" with "in all kinds of weather." But Sadie wanted to rhyme it with "our jungle is better." I said we should add another verse so we could sing it both ways.

When Isabel turned left toward the tortoise, Sadie turned right toward the spiny anteater. When Sadie wanted to stare at the giraffes for longer, Isabel was eager to move on to the camels. When Sadie sat on a bench to watch the tiger prowl, Isabel stood near the fence. I ran back and forth between them and barely saw the tiger at all.

I felt like they were playing a game of tug-of-war and I was the rope.

Playing tug-of-war with Banana is fun. Sadie and Isabel playing tug-of-war over me was not. This was not how I'd thought the field trip would go.

Before Sadie and I met Isabel, I always went along with what Sadie wanted, or Sadie went along with me. It was easy for us to agree on things. Now that I had two best friends, it was more complicated. I couldn't agree with them both, but I didn't want to choose sides, either. I didn't want anyone's feelings to get hurt. I just wanted to keep everyone happy.

Sadie and Isabel didn't look unhappy right that minute, so I guessed I was doing an okay job. But it was like walking on a balance beam. I knew that if I wasn't careful, I could fall off at any second. All it would take was one wrong step.

We followed Leticia up a bamboo-lined path to where the panda bears lived. I squeezed Isabel's hand. I knew she'd been waiting for this moment all day. But then I saw Sadie looking at my hand in Isabel's and I quickly let go. I didn't want to make Sadie jealous.

I'd thought all panda bears were black and white, but the first sign we came to said RED PANDAS. I looked out into the treetops and spotted a fuzzy, fox-colored animal curled up on a branch, enjoying the sun. He had a long bushy tail and an adorable face.

"I want one!" Sadie said. "Wouldn't he look great in my room?"

"He looks like my cat," Isabel said. Isabel's cat, Mewsic, is a gigantic orange tabby who's even bigger than Banana. Isabel named him Mewsic because he loves listening when Isabel's sister Maria plays the cello.

Sadie tilted her head, studying the red panda. "Sort of," she said. "He looks more like a raccoon, though. Right, Anna?" She and Isabel both turned to look at me.

"He does look like Mewsic," I said. Isabel beamed. Sadie frowned. "But with a raccoon tail," I added. "So you're both right."

Before they could argue about it more, I distracted them by saying, "Let's go find the giant panda!" Luckily, it worked.

The black-and-white giant panda didn't look so giant because he was all the way at the back of his pen, munching slowly on some bamboo leaves. We took turns watching him through the binoculars.

"Ooh, he's so cute!" I said when it was my turn to look at him. "Even cuter than in the videos we saw. And he looks just as soft as Banana."

Isabel nodded happily. But Sadie didn't look convinced. "Let me see," she said. I stepped aside and she put her face up to the binoculars. She looked for a minute, then shrugged. "I don't think he's cuter than the zebras," she said.

Suddenly my face felt as warm as it had in the tropical parrot jungle. "That's not what I said!" I protested. "Besides, it's not a competition."

"You like the pandas though, right?" Isabel asked. "You just said you did."

"I love all animals," I explained, trying to reassure them both.

"What's your favorite animal, though?" Sadie asked. It sounded like a normal question, but it felt like a test. I wasn't sure how to answer. But there was no getting out of it.

"Banana!" I finally said. Which was true, of course.

"No, what's your favorite zoo animal?" Sadie said. "Which do you like better, zebras or pandas?"

If felt like she was asking which I liked better, Sadies or Isabels. It felt like she'd been wondering that all day long.

My heart was beating faster than a bumblebee's wings. How could I convince Sadie that Isabel was not her replacement? How could I get her to stop expecting me to choose? "I like the elephants!" I blurted. "The elephants are my favorite so far."

Sadie nodded and I thought I was off the hook. But then Isabel pushed, "If you had to choose between pandas and zebras, what would you say?"

I looked at Sadie, standing on one side of me with her arms crossed, and Isabel on the other, her eyes filled with hope. I couldn't take it anymore. "Stop it!" I yelled. "You're making me feel like the monkey in the middle!"

Chapter Eleven

Who's the Fairest?

Isabel and Sadie looked stunned. "Sorry, Anna," Isabel said gently, like she was afraid the words might break me. "We didn't mean to do that."

"Yeah," Sadie said, uncrossing her arms. "We weren't doing it on purpose. We were just having fun." But I knew it was more than that.

I took a deep breath and let out the truth. "Well, it's not fun for me," I said. "I don't want us to argue about every little thing. You have to stop asking me to choose between you."

Sadie's cheeks went pink. "It's hard with three of us sometimes," she said, "when one of us gets

left out, or worried we will be. I'm not used to having to share my best friend."

My heart leaped for Sadie. I didn't want her to feel left out. I didn't want any of us to feel that way. "Maybe we need a system," I said.

"A system for deciding who's right?" Isabel asked.

"No," I said. "A system for making sure everything is fair. Like how we'll take turns being the one who has to sit with someone else on the bus."

Sadie was nodding. "Yeah, we need rules. We should promise to share things equally and decide everything together."

Relief rushed through me. I was glad Sadie

understood what I was talking about. And Sadie has always been good at making up rules.

"What about when one of us wants something different from what the others want?" Isabel asked.

"We can't let that happen," Sadie explained. "We all have to do everything exactly the same. Then no one will feel left out or get stuck in the middle."

Isabel looked unsure whether that was a good idea, like how Banana looks when I try to feed her celery. But after a pause, she said, "Okay. That does sound most fair."

"Yeah! It's a plan. This will be great," I said. "Three cheers for triplets!" I bumped my hip against Isabel's to make her laugh, then bumped against Sadie's, too, to make it fair.

"The best things come in threes," Sadie said. "Like us."

"We'll be like the Three Musketeers. *All for one and one for all*," Isabel said.

I heard Justin snicker as he and Timothy came over to use the panda binoculars. "Or the three *mouse*-keteers," Justin said. He held up his hands like tiny paws and wiggled his nose. "Eek, eek, eek!" he said in what I guess was supposed to be a mouse voice. He reminded me more of Banana's squeaky rabbit.

"That doesn't even make sense," I said. I held my chin high and turned away from him. Sadie and Isabel did the same. At least we could all agree that Justin was being dumb.

It seemed like a good start.

Chapter Twelve
No Fair, No Fun

We said good-bye to the pandas and followed Leticia and Ms. Burland to the lunch area. Mr. Garrison's class and Ms. Chung's class were already there, spread out at the picnic tables. Sadie ran ahead to claim us a good spot, so we wouldn't get separated.

Isabel slid onto the bench next to Sadie, and I plopped down across from them. My tummy rumbled as I pulled my lunch bag out of my back-pack. "Did you hear that?" I said. "My stomach is growling like a bear."

"Mine's roaring like a lion," Sadie said. She

was taking everything out of her lunchbox and placing it neatly on the table. Sadie likes things organized, even when she's hungry.

"Mine just purred like a kitten," Isabel said with her mouth full. Sadie and I giggled at that, but Isabel didn't mind. She's almost never embarrassed. "It's happy because I'm already feeding it," she explained, and took another big bite of her sandwich.

I peeked into my bag and saw the special surprise I'd brought for my friends. I'd almost forgotten about it. Now I was extra glad that I had enough to share. "I got us a treat," I said. "Fruit strips for everyone!"

"Yum," Isabel said, reaching for one. "Thanks!" Luckily Dad had packed three of the same flavor, so we didn't have to fight over who got which kind.

"I'll share my raisins," Sadie said, shaking the box. She poured out a pile for each of us. We both looked at Isabel. "You should share something too," Sadie said. "Then it's fair, right?"

Isabel pulled her string cheese into three equal parts, and handed one piece to Sadie and one to me. I bit into the cheese and felt it squeak between my teeth.

I chewed happily. Sharing felt good. This new system was way better than fighting or worrying.

I couldn't wait to tell Banana how my idea had saved the day.

"So what animal should we do our report on?" Isabel asked.

Sadie had her mouth full of peanut butter, so I spoke up first. "I was thinking we should do it on giant pandas. We could talk about how they're endangered and might go extinct."

"That sounds perfect!" Isabel said, folding a strand of cheese into a heart.

But Sadie swallowed hard. "I want us to do it on zebras," she said. "Or the miniature horses."

I considered that. "I love horses," I said. "And zebras, too. But the pandas are special because there aren't very many of them, especially in the wild. And if people don't do something about it, soon there won't be any left at all."

"It's so sad," Isabel said. "We need to protect them."

"We can't do our project on pandas," Sadie said, putting down her sandwich. "That's not following the rules."

"What rules?" Isabel said.

"*Our* rules," Sadie said. "We promised to do everything fairly."

I thought about how to make it fair. "Maybe we should vote on it," I suggested.

Sadie shook her head. "Then you guys will both vote for pandas and I won't really get a say. That's not fair to me."

"Choosing zebras isn't fair for everyone either," Isabel pointed out.

"Right," Sadie said. "Exactly. So we have to choose an animal that's nobody's favorite."

They both went quiet.

"Okay," I said. "So, what do we all like equally?

Otters?" Isabel frowned. "Sloths?" I suggested. Sadie wrinkled her nose.

"How about crocodiles?" Isabel said. "We all liked those okay."

I looked at Sadie. She looked at Isabel. Isabel looked at me.

I stared down at my fruit strip. It didn't have any better solutions. "I guess so," I said.

"Fine," Sadie agreed.

"Crocodiles it is, then," Isabel said. She didn't sound excited about it either.

I still wanted to do our report on pandas.

The things we had learned about them were really interesting, and I knew it would make a cool project. But as my Nana sometimes says, you can't always get what you want.

At least we were all equally disappointed. That was fair . . . right?

Chapter Thirteen
Walky-Talky

On the bus ride back to school I slid into a seat with Isabel like I'd promised, and Sadie took the seat right in front of us. She tried turning around to talk with us a couple of times, but after getting yelled at twice by the bus driver, she gave up and stayed facing forward. Luckily we knew it would be a short trip.

Isabel took out a book and we huddled close so we could read it together. When she was ready to turn a page, she nodded once to show she was done, and waited for me to finish too. I didn't race to keep up though. I just read at my own pace. I knew Isabel wouldn't judge me for being slower.

It was a good book with ballerinas in it, and I wished Sadie could be read-ing it too. But as we reached the school parking lot, I heard her laughing with her  seatmate, Jesmyn, who was in Ms. Dandino's class with us last year. And she was all smiles as the three of us got off the bus and said good-bye. I hoped there'd be someone nice like Jesmyn on our next trip, when it would be my turn to be the one to sit apart.

When I got home, Banana was waiting for me at the door. She wanted to hear all about the zoo, and she also wanted a walk. I clipped her leash onto her collar and we set out around the block.

As we walked, I told Banana about the animals I'd seen, from the fuzzy little baby monkey that was riding on its mother's back to the yellow-and-black leopard gecko that can shed its tail and grow a new one if it gets caught by a predator. Banana and I agreed that was a pretty cool trick.

I described the rain-forest aquariums where the tree frogs live, and how the Monkey House smells like Chuck's room, only ten times worse.

I told her how we got to hear a lion roar, and Isabel roared back. Then Sadie and I did it too, and Isabel and Sadie got into a contest over who could do it better, and wanted me to judge.

Banana looked worried. I guess she could tell where this was going.

"They weren't fighting, exactly," I said. "Not really. But they were definitely fighting for my attention. I wish . . ." I sighed instead of finishing the thought. Banana nudged at my leg with her nose. I crouched down to pat her.

"I know I'm lucky to have two best friends," I said. "But sometimes it feels like I'm a prize they're competing for, or a toy they're tossing back and forth."

Banana wagged her tail hopefully at the word "toy." That made me smile a little.

"I worry that Sadie and Isabel are always wondering which of them I like best," I said. "But I love them both. It's like that rule we learned in math class, 'You can't compare apples and oranges.' I can't compare Sadies and Isabels. It's like comparing apples and orangutans, or apes and oranges. How do you choose a favorite? They're completely different things."

Banana put her two front paws on my knee, and leaned in to lick my face. I giggled and pulled back. She barked and licked me again

insistently, like she was trying to tell me something important.

"Don't worry," I said, lifting her floppy ears so
they flew out to the sides like Dumbo's. "You'll
always be my favorite Banana."

Chapter Fourteen

You Choose, You Lose

Chuck was in a good mood at dinner because his math test hadn't been so hard after all, and because Dad and I had made tacos. Chuck loves tacos. Banana loves taco night too, because it's very hard to bite into a taco without spilling its insides out the other end. Lots of yummy nibbles always drop to the floor for her to eat, especially around my chair. I'd already given her some kibble for dinner, but Banana thinks people food is most delicious.

Dad asked Mom how her important meeting went, and Mom talked for a while about "visual impact" and "staying on message" and "increased market demand." I only half listened while piling beans, corn, lettuce, and tomato into my next taco shell. I sprinkled shredded cheese over the top and smooshed it down, trying to seal in all the other layers. I took a bite. A bean escaped. Banana lunged for it.

Mom loves talking with Dad about work stuff. She calls it "strategizing." Strategizing is like planning, and my parents are big into plans. I thought about telling them Sadie's and Isabel's and my plan for making sure everything is exactly equal and fair, and how it worked really well except for when it maybe sort of didn't, but there wasn't a good moment to interrupt. My parents are not big into interrupting.

Finally, Mom asked how my day went and I told them about all the animals I'd met. "I think I might want to be a zookeeper when I grow up," I said. "Since I love taking care of animals. That seems even funner than being a vet."

"Oh yeah?" Dad said.

"Yeah. And Banana can come to work with me. She'll hang out at the petting zoo and get belly rubs from the visitors. And I'll train the monkeys to throw her toys so she can play fetch with them when I'm busy."

"I bet you'd be an excellent zookeeper," Mom said. "You certainly have a way with animals. Right, Banana?"

Banana wagged yes and went under Mom's chair to see if she'd dropped anything.

As Chuck and I cleared the table, Dad

announced that he'd gotten us a special treat for dessert. "I couldn't resist when I saw the name of it," he said. "It's called monkey bread!"

I giggled. "What's monkey bread?" I asked.

"It's a kind of cake," Dad said, "made with cinnamon and caramel and yeasty dough. Try it. I think you'll like it." He opened the bakery box and took out two slices. "They're big, so I got one piece for Mom and me, and one for you and Chuck. You each get half."

"I claim the bigger half!" Chuck said.

Mom shook her head. "You know the drill," she said. "One person cuts, the other one chooses."

"I'll cut," I said quickly. "I'm sick of choosing." I'd had enough of that already today.

I sliced the monkey bread as close to down the middle as I could. It was gooey and soft, which made it hard to cut perfectly. Banana watched me with huge, hopeful eyes, like that might convince me to cut a third piece for her. I was tempted.

One piece was slightly bigger, and Chuck reached out to take it. "Wait!" I said, lifting the plate to keep it away from him. I wanted to make a second cut to even out the pieces. But Chuck grabbed at it again. I jerked it away and before I could steady the plate, the smaller piece slid off and dropped straight into Banana's mouth.

Chapter Fifteen
Gobble-Gobble

"Oh no!" I cried as the monkey bread fell.

Banana couldn't believe her luck. She gobbled up the treat, practically swallowing it whole, before anyone could take it away from her. No one even tried.

"Look what you did!" Chuck yelled.

"Me? You did that!" I yelled back.

"You were holding the plate!" he said.

"You grabbed it and threw me off balance!" I said.

"*You* dropped it!" Chuck shouted.

"*Arrrrrgh!*" I screamed. I was so frustrated, I couldn't even use words.

"That's enough, both of you," Mom said. "If you keep this up, I'm going to give Banana the other half too."

I clamped my mouth shut. Chuck's jaw dropped open. "You wouldn't," he said.

Mom crossed her arms. "Try me," she said.

I couldn't handle any more of this. I pushed the plate toward Chuck. "Here," I said. "It's your slice. You called it. Just take it."

Chuck looked suspicious. "What's wrong with it?" he asked, eyeing the cake.

"Nothing!" I said. I blinked hard, hoping I wouldn't cry. "I'm just trying to be nice. I'm sick of bending over backwards to make everything fair, and everyone feeling left out and unhappy and fighting anyway. So I'll just be the one left out and you can eat the stupid monkey bread. I don't care. I give up."

My family held very still, like they thought the slightest movement might cause me to explode.

They may have been right.

Finally, Chuck took the plate. He picked up the knife from the table and cut the piece of monkey bread in two. "Here," he said, handing me half. "We can share it."

I took the treat with one hand and wiped a tear from my face with the other. "Thanks," I said.

Chuck nodded. I took a small bite. Monkey bread was delicious.

Chapter Sixteen

Fairer Than Fair

After dessert, Mom and Chuck were on dish-washing duty, so Banana and I went into the living room to curl up on the couch with a book. It was hard to concentrate on reading, though. The words seemed to be swimming around on the pages and I couldn't make them stay put. Even when I managed to catch a few, they wouldn't sit still in my head.

Dad came in and patted Banana's rump, then patted me on the head. He sank into his favorite armchair. "Feeling any better?" he asked.

I shrugged.

He raised an eyebrow. "You want to talk about it, kiddo?"

I ran my hand over Banana's soft ears and wondered how to even explain what was going on. "Isabel and Sadie are making me feel like monkey bread," I said.

Dad pressed his lips together. "How so?" he asked.

I told him what had happened on the bus and at the zoo, and how it felt like Isabel and Sadie were sort of fighting over me. "I'm trying to divide myself equally, but it seems like they both keep thinking they're getting the smaller piece."

"Wow," Dad said. "That sounds exhausting."

"It is!" I said. "And it feels impossible to make everyone happy."

"Well, that's because it *is* impossible to make everyone happy," Dad said. "But you know, fairness doesn't always mean everyone gets the same thing."

That surprised me. "What?" I said.

Dad leaned forward. "What I mean is, there are some things that it's good to try to split evenly.

Like a cookie, or maybe even who sits next to whom on the bus."

I nodded. "That's what we're doing."

"Right," Dad said. "But things like friendship and love don't work that way. You, my dear, are not a cookie, and your friendship is not a piece of cake. Having two best friends doesn't mean cutting yourself in half to hand out two smaller pieces. Your love doesn't get divided up like monkey bread. It grows and grows, like the pasta in Strega Nona's magic pot."

"I know that," I said. And I did. But I wished I could explain it to Isabel and Sadie.

Dad scratched the back of his neck, like he sometimes does when he's thinking. "It sounds like you and Sadie and Isabel came up with a pretty good system for how to make things work today. And you'll keep on figuring out what works. But not everything will always be equal, and that's okay. In fact, sometimes it's *more* fair that way."

"How could that be more fair?" I said. "That makes no sense."

"Well, for example, is it unfair that I wear glasses and you and Mom and Chuck don't have any?" Dad said.

"Um . . . no?" I said.

Dad didn't seem to notice that he'd lost me. "I think being fair means making sure everyone has what they need," he said. "Which is not the same thing as giving everyone what they *want*, by the way. And since everyone has different needs, the things we get aren't always the same. Like how I need glasses but the rest of you don't, so

I get glasses and you do not. It would be silly to hand out glasses to everyone because one person needs them. And it would be even sillier to say that I can't have glasses because the rest of you aren't wearing any."

Huh. I hadn't thought of it that way.

"Fairness doesn't always mean sameness," Dad went on. "But if you're looking for things to be unfair, you'll probably always find it. So I think an important part of friendship is not keeping score. You have to trust that things will even out in the long run."

I almost laughed. "Yeah, but what if Sadie and Isabel keep score? They keep asking me what I think and wanting me to make choices about stuff."

Dad shrugged. "So tell them what you think.

Maybe they really want to hear your opinion. They're your friends, Anna. They want you to be you. It's okay if you don't all think the same thing. In fact, it's probably a lot more interesting that way."

Banana nuzzled up against me to show she agreed.

I took a deep breath, and let it out fast. "Okay," I said. "I'll try it."

"Good," Dad said. He smiled. "You know what I think would be fair *and* fun? Let's invite Isabel and Sadie for a sleepover this weekend."

I sat up fast, startling Banana. "Really?" I said.

"Yup," Dad said. I tackled him with a hug and he laughed and squeezed me back. "I'll call their parents. You go brush your teeth. Mom will be up soon to tuck you in."

I started up the stairs. "And hey, Anna," Dad called after me.

I stopped. "Yeah?" I said.

"No monkey business."

Chapter Seventeen
Let Me Count the Ways

I woke up super early with the morning sunlight flooding into my room and an idea flooding into my brain. I finally got what Banana had been trying to tell me on our walk yesterday. I heard the shower turn on in my parents' bathroom, which meant Mom was getting ready and Dad was probably already up. I couldn't wait to tell him my idea. I threw on some clothes and ran downstairs with Banana right beside me. "Dad!" I shouted as we burst into the kitchen. There was no response.

Banana led the way to the other side of the

house, where Dad's office is. The door was closed and I could hear the *tap-tap-tap* of his fingers on the keyboard. Dad must have woken up with ideas in his brain too.

The books Dad writes are really long and they're all set in the past. The covers show women in dresses that lace up the front and men whose shirts are blowing off in the wind. In the background there's a sunset or a storm, and sometimes a ship or a castle. The man and the woman usually look like they're angry or about to kiss. Possibly both.

Chuck says the books have a lot of kissing in them.

Some of the covers have horses on them too, like the last one, *Heart's Full Gallop*. I liked it when Dad was writing that one because he needed me to tell him everything I know about horses to help with his research. Sadie says we should read that one when we're older. But even though it has a white stallion on the cover, I think it's still mostly about the kissing.

It's nice that Dad being a writer means he's always home and available if we need him, but I know better than to interrupt him when he's on a roll. Besides, this was an emergency I could handle myself. I just needed to find my glitter pens.

Banana and I tiptoed away from the office door so we wouldn't disturb Dad's work. We searched for the glitter pens in the living room, in my bedroom, and in Mom's huge walk-in closet. There was no sign of them. I was about to send

Banana to sneak a look in Chuck's bedroom, when I remembered using the glitter pens in the kitchen to make a card for Nana and Grumps last week. We found them in the regular pen jar on the counter. Dad had used the green one to write *More coffee* on the grocery list.

I rescued the sparkly pens and found some pretty blue paper that I was sure Mom would say I could use for this if she were out of the shower to ask. But I didn't have time to wait. And I only needed two pieces: one for each of my two best friends.

I sat down with my supplies at the kitchen table and Banana sat nearby to watch. I uncapped the silver glitter pen and, in my very best printing, wrote *You Are My Favorite Isabel Because* across the top of the first sheet of paper. Then I chose the purple glitter pen and wrote *You Are My Favorite Sadie Because* on the other sheet.

I showed Banana. She thumped her tail.

We made two different lists for my two different best friends, to show them why they could never be replaced.

I was just putting the finishing touches on my lists when Mom walked into the kitchen. She peeked over my shoulder at the border of rainbows and ponies that I was drawing around Sadie's list. I'm not as great an artist as Isabel, but it still looked really good. "That's beautiful, Annabear," Mom said. "I like the hearts and stars and squiggles on the other one, too. Is this for homework?"

"Nope," I said. "It's for choosing favorites. A favorite Isabel and a favorite Sadie."

"Oh," Mom said. "Well, want to help your favorite mother put out the breakfast things when you're done?"

"Sure!" I said. I used the gold pen to draw a tiny dog at the bottom of Sadie's list, like I'd already done on Isabel's. I wrote, *P.S. You're Banana's favorite Sadie too.*

There. The lists were done.

Now each of my favorite friends would know she'd never be second best.

Chapter Eighteen

Three Heads Are
Better Than One

When I got to school, Isabel and Sadie were already there. I spotted them out on the playground, dangling off the monkey bars. It looked like they were practicing some kind of fancy gymnastics routine they must have made up together that morning. I was glad to see them getting along so well without me. They might not be best friends yet, but they were definitely having fun.

"Anna!" Isabel shouted when she saw me. I ran over to them.

"We're doing flips," Sadie said. "Watch!"

Sadie counted to three, and she and Isabel swung their legs in the air and hooked their knees around the bars. They let go with their hands and dangled upside down with their arms stretched out.

I clapped. "Bravo!" I cheered, like I'd seen people do on TV.

They laughed and jumped down. "Who did it faster?" Sadie asked, fixing her ponytail.

"Isabel did," I said honestly.

I watched to see if Sadie might get mad, but she didn't look upset. Maybe Dad was right. Maybe she really wasn't keeping score. "Let's do it again!" she said, climbing back up.

Isabel nudged me. "Your turn to try it. This time I'll be the judge."

I wriggled out of my backpack and tucked in my shirt. We flipped and climbed and twisted through the air until the first bell rang.

As we walked toward the school building, I took out the lists I'd made and handed them to my friends.

"What's this?" Sadie asked, unfolding hers.

"Pretty," Isabel said, touching the border I'd drawn.

Sadie's smile got wider and wider as she read hers. She threw her arms around my neck. "You're my favorite Anna, too," she said.

"And mine," Isabel said, joining the hug. "I'm going to hang this in my room!"

I felt as pleased as a dog with two tails, as my Nana would say.

We stepped into the classroom and went to our seats. I looked up at the whiteboard. The word of the day was "lionhearted." *Lionhearted: brave and determined; courageous*. I liked that.

Ms. Burland clapped twice to start the day. "Good morning, junior zoologists!" she said. "Today we're heading straight for the library to work on our animal reports. Grab your partner or partners, and a notebook and pen, and let's line up at the door, please!"

I reached into my desk and took out my lucky blue pencil and the purple notebook with the three pony stickers on it. I hoped they would give me luck in telling my friends what I'd decided I needed to say. I'd rehearsed it with Banana that morning, but I was still worried the words might not come out right. Or that Sadie might be upset when she heard them.

Sadie was saving Isabel and me a place at the front of the line, right behind Ms. Burland. "Are those real fur?" Sadie asked Ms. Burland as we followed her down the hall.

I looked down at the teacher's feet. Her shoes were covered in leopard-print fur. They made a *click, click, clack* sound as she walked.

"Nope!" Ms. Burland said. "No giant cats—or tiny ones—were harmed in the making of these shoes. They're pretty wild, though, right?"

Sadie giggled. "Ferocious feet," she said.

"Rwarrr!" Isabel added.

We claimed a small table in one corner of the library. Isabel uncapped her pen. "Okay, so, crocodiles," she said. "What if we—"

"Wait," I said, at the exact same time that Sadie said it too.

We looked at each other. "You first," Sadie said.

I sat up as tall as I could go and tried to be as lionhearted as possible. "I think we should do our project on giant pandas," I said. "Sadie, I know you think that's unfair, but everything can't always be fair, and—"

"No," Sadie interrupted. "I think we should do it on pandas too."

I was so surprised, I couldn't speak.

"You do?" Isabel said.

"Yeah." Sadie nodded. "Crocodiles are all right, but pandas are way cooler. I still don't think they're as great as zebras, but they're really cute, and Isabel, I know you love them." She turned to me. "Like you said, it's sad that they're endangered. People should talk about that. *We* should talk about that. It will make a great report."

"Cool," Isabel said.

"Okay," I agreed. I felt my smile reaching all the way up to my eyes. "Let's do it."

"I think we should make a poster to go with the presentation," Sadie said. "Isabel can draw the pandas, and I'm pretty good at trees. Anna, you have the nicest handwriting, so you should do the lettering."

"Yeah!" Isabel said. "And we can glue cotton balls onto the pandas so they're actually fuzzy, like Ms. Burland's shoes."

"And we'll use black markers to color in some of the cotton balls," I added.

"We should write all this down," Sadie said.

Isabel wrote *Ideas* at the top of her paper and started making a list. "This is going to be an awesome project," she said. Sadie and I agreed.

"Hey, maybe your dad will let us make panda pancakes at the sleepover this weekend," Sadie said to me.

The sleepover! Banana and I couldn't wait. "I bet he will," I said.

I grinned at my favorite Isabel and my favorite Sadie. We made a great team.

Acknowledgments

Thank you to:

Editor extraordinaire and friend
of all pandas Kristin Ostby;

art director Laurent Linn, illustrator Meg Park,
and the whole talented herd at S&S;

zookeeper—nay, shepherd
of dreams Meredith Kaffel Simonoff;

my pack, especially plot wrangler Robin Wasserman,
lion tamer Terra McVoy, and slugabed Jeff Snyder;

Jeremy, Anna, and Pia, who took me to the zoo;

my parents, who appreciate strange birds
and silly geese;

Arugula Badidea, who is very ferocious;
and my flock of fellow book lovers.

And now, a sneak peek
at the next book in the series,
*ANNA, BANANA, AND
THE BIG-MOUTH BET*

Anna, Banana, and the Big-Mouth Bet

Anica Mrose Rissi ILLUSTRATED BY Meg Park

That Spells Trouble

Trouble, I wrote, spelling it out in my head as I printed the word on the test. *T-r-o-u-b-l-e*.

O-plus-*U* and *L*-before-*E* were the hard parts in that one, but I was certain I'd gotten it right. Dad had quizzed me on all the spelling and vocabulary words this morning at breakfast, and even Banana was amazed by how quickly I'd breezed through them. And dogs are hardly ever impressed by good spelling.

I tapped my lucky blue pencil against my lip as I thought about how to use the word in a sentence. *Banana once got in trouble for chewing*

Chuck's sneaker, I wrote, wrinkling my nose at the memory. Banana doesn't chew on things she's not supposed to anymore, but she still loves sniffing at things that stink, including my older brother's yucky shoes.

"Pesky!" our teacher, Ms. Burland, exclaimed. She always sings out the words for our tests as though she's performing them onstage. It makes the quizzes a lot more dramatic, and even kind of fun. "Pesky," she repeated, this time in a low, booming voice. Beside me, my best friend Isabel giggled.

I wrote down the word, then used it in a sentence: *Those pesky flies won't leave us alone!*

I glanced over at my other best friend, Sadie. I knew she'd been nervous about the test, so I was worried for her. But Sadie was bent over her paper, scribbling the answer, with her curls spilling into her face. It looked like she was doing fine.

"No cheating, Anna!" Justin called out from the desk behind mine. My mouth fell open and my heart sped up at the attack. I wasn't cheating!

Ms. Burland raised her eyebrows in our direction. "You should all have your eyes on your own papers, please," she said.

I looked down quickly. I wasn't really in trouble, but my cheeks still burned. Forget flies—I should have written my sentence about pesky Justin. He was the worst.

"Accuse," Ms. Burland announced, sounding stern. "Accuse!" she repeated, calling it out like a cheerful greeting.

I narrowed my eyes. *Justin likes to accuse innocent girls of cheating*, I wrote on my test. There. That ought to clear my name. And I hoped Ms. Burland would notice that I'd also used one of last week's spelling words, "innocent," and spelled it correctly. I thought that was pretty clever of me.

But wait, was "cheat-ing" spelled right? I pressed my lips together, thinking hard, and gasped. I'd felt a tooth move! I touched the tooth with my tongue and pushed  it again. Sure enough, it wiggled.

I was so distracted by the slightly loose tooth, I almost missed the final spelling word. Luckily, Ms. Burland said it once more. "About."

I spelled it out carefully and wrote, *I can't wait to tell Banana and Sadie and Isabel about my loose tooth!*

Loosey-Goosey

When the test was over, Ms. Burland asked Isabel and Timothy to collect all the papers. I put my lucky blue pencil that I use for quizzes back down on the desk, in between the regular pencil I use for normal schoolwork and the supersparkly rainbow pencil I hardly use at all. The supersparkly rainbow pencil is mostly too special to write with, but I love to look at it. Sadie gave it to me after the one I'd had before it broke.

I peeked over at Sadie and lifted both eyebrows to ask, *How'd the test go?* Sadie grinned and gave me a thumbs-up.

Usually Theresa, the housekeeper at Sadie's mom's place, helps Sadie study for spelling tests. But this week Theresa was away on vacation and Sadie was staying at her dad's house, and he's not as good as my dad or Theresa at quiz prep. He does buy us really tasty snacks for sleepovers, though. And he lets us drink soda and watch TV, and doesn't get mad about pillow fights.

There's no soda allowed at my house, and it's hard to get away with a late-night pillow fight because Banana gets excited and wakes everyone up with her barking. Though my dad said even if Banana hadn't barked, he still would have heard Sadie and Isabel and me shrieking and giggling at the sleepover last weekend. Now that I have two best friends, we make a lot more noise than when I only had one.

The bell rang for recess and we lined up to follow Ms. Burland down the hall. Sadie, Isabel, and I ran straight for the small merry-go-round as soon as we got outside. Usually third graders don't go on the small merry-go-round because it's made for little kids, but we wanted to play a new game Isabel had invented called Spin Me a Tale.

The game is, one person sits in the center of the merry-go-round and holds on to the bars while the other two spin her around. As the person is spinning, she has to make up a story and tell it really quick, before the merry-go-round slows to a stop. But spinning on the merry-go-round makes our brains dizzy, so the stories usually come out pretty silly.

If someone shouts "Switch!" we spin the merry-go-round in the other direction, and the storyteller has to switch something important about the story—the evil fairy becomes good, or the puppy turns into a goose, or the princess doesn't want to marry the prince after all. Switch is my favorite part.

Yesterday I made up a story about Banana chasing a squirrel made of cheese, and when

Isabel yelled "Switch!" I changed it to the cheese chasing Banana. We laughed so hard that Isabel snorted. Justin heard the snort and started making piggy noises, which only made Isabel laugh even harder, but Sadie still told him to go away. Sadie likes Justin and sometimes giggles at his jokes, but she doesn't like anyone making fun of her friends.

I felt like Justin had been giving us an extra-hard time this week. I wished I knew how to get him to bug off.

"Whose turn is it?" Isabel asked as we reached the merry-go-round. We try to take turns and be fair with games and stuff.

"Mine!" Sadie said, climbing into the middle.

"Wait," I said. "I have something to show you. Look!" I dropped open my jaw and wiggled the loose tooth with my finger. It was a bottom tooth—one of the extra-pointy ones.

"Oooooh, loose tooth!" Isabel said.

Sadie peered in closer. "I don't see anything," she said.

"It isn't super loose yet," I explained. "But it will be."

Isabel bounced on her toes. Her face was full of excitement. "I wonder what the Tooth Fairy will bring you," she said.

I shrugged. "I usually get a few coins and a treat, like sparkly stickers or a cool hair tie."

"Isn't it funny how the Tooth Fairy brings different things to different houses?" Isabel said. "I always get a letter with my prize, but my friend Cassie from Ms. Lahiri's class last year only gets money. Maybe it's because I leave the Tooth Fairy a note and a drawing along with my tooth, so she writes back."

I squinted at her. Sometimes it's hard to tell if Isabel is joking. Chuck had told Sadie and me the truth about the Tooth Fairy years ago. Surely Isabel's big sisters would have told her by now too. But Isabel looked completely serious.

I glanced at Sadie, expecting her to inform Isabel that there is no Tooth Fairy, but Sadie went with it. "The Tooth Fairy comes to *both* my houses," she said. "Last time I got money under the pillow at my mom's house and a whole box of chocolate caramels plus a letter at my dad's."

I remembered those chocolates. They'd been

delicious. Sadie and I had shared one every day for the next two weeks, at whatever random moment Sadie had declared it to be Chocolate
Time. That was before we became friends with Isabel. I've known Sadie forever, but we only just met Isabel in Ms. Burland's class this year.

If Sadie wasn't going to say anything to Isabel about the Tooth Fairy, then I wouldn't either. But it was kind of embarrassing that she didn't know the truth.

"Let's play the game," I said to change the subject. I'd spotted our classmates Amanda and Keisha skipping rope nearby. They didn't look like they were listening to us, but I didn't want to risk them overhearing. If they caught on that Isabel still believed in the Tooth Fairy, they might think she was babyish. What if they thought I was babyish too?

Not that it mattered what Amanda thought—she sometimes picks her nose in public—but who knew who she'd tell. If Justin found out, he would never let us hear the end of it. The last thing we needed was more teasing from him.

"Spin me!" Sadie commanded.

Isabel and I grabbed on to the merry-go-round and the story began.